I0569904

GRIM REPO

GRIM REPO FILES

MARK FASSETT

OTHER BOOKS BY MARK FASSETT

The Sacrifice of Mendleson Moony

A Wizard's Work
Shattered
* Fragments
* Reworked

Lords of Genova
Questioner's Shadow

Novellas & Novelettes
Zombies Ate My Mom

* Forthcoming

GRIM REPO

GRIM REPO FILES

MARK FASSETT

RAVENSTAR PRESS
MONROE, WA

Published 2012 by Ravenstar Press
Monroe, WA
http://www.ravenstarpress.com

This is a work of fiction. All characters appearing in this work are fictitious. Any resemblance to real persons, living or dead is purely conincidental.

Trade paper edition designed by Mark Fassett
in Scribus

Electronic editions designed by Mark Fassett
using StoryBox software
http://www.markfassett.com
http://www.storyboxsoftware.com

Cover design: Mark Fassett
Image © Philcold | Dreamstime.com

ISBN: 978-0615697451

ACKNOWLEDGEMENTS

I want to say thank you to the people that helped me with getting this book ready for you to read. Rebecca M. Senese, David Michael, Michael Canfield, and Michael Kingswood were all instrumental in making Grim Repo better. Any remaining errors are my fault.

I also need to thank my wife, Wendy, who reads everything I write, even though none of what I write is her preferred genre.

·· 1 ··

Pain. I had known pain for as long as I could remember. I'm sure I knew it even before I could remember, all the way back to the day I was born, when I shot out from my mother's womb with my arm broken.

My father once told me I was already screaming. That they didn't need to spank my ass to get me going.

"Grimm, are you alive in there?"

The voice came from outside my head, outside the memories, outside the pitch black cocoon I had sealed myself inside.

I didn't respond. I couldn't.

"Grimm? Make a noise if you're alive."

I even recognized Alice's voice, the subtle timbre that spoke of love and kindness and things I didn't understand. But no. Those weren't there. She was a Synth.

I tried to kick for her, but I couldn't move. The cocoon had collapsed on me in the crash. They weren't supposed to do that. Centat Systems claimed they could survive a three hundred gravity collision and keep the occupant alive.

Maybe it had done that. After all, I still lived.

But I couldn't move enough to make a sound Alice could hear with her ears. If she had been using a listening device, she should have heard my breather, my heartbeat.

That she wasn't using a device only meant that things were bad outside my cocoon.

I tried, anyway. I attempted to strike out with my right arm, the one limb that didn't feel broken or crushed, but I couldn't move it more than a centimeter. The protective gel held me too tight.

I heard two thumps against the exterior of the cocoon.

"Open it up," Alice said.

I don't know why I could hear her at all. The protective gel should have kept the noise from reaching me. Don't get me wrong. I wasn't complaining.

"I don't care if you think it's a waste of time. Grimm might still be alive in there, and I want it open."

Thank you, Alice.

One of the problems with the cocoons is that they're difficult to open. They're made that way to protect the occupant. Once the cocoon is sealed, the cocoon won't open for anything except its own electronics or some seriously heavy duty cutting tools. The electronics had to be smashed, or the unlock mechanism damaged. Most likely, both, or they wouldn't have had to resort to yelling through the cocoon wall.

I just hoped that when they cut me open they didn't cut my leg off. I didn't want to spend three months growing yet another leg, or worse. I could tell the damage was already bad enough.

The only thing keeping me alive was the breathing tube that had jammed itself just a little too far down my throat. I wanted to cough, but even that was impossible.

The whine came through tiny and tinny at first when they started up the saw. It must have been Mickey. I hoped it was Mickey.

And then the real sound and light show began as the saw cut into the outer shell. I knew, outside, sparks would be flying everywhere. Inside, the gel stopped them, but I could still see the light, a bright blue flame. The first light I had seen in three days.

Three days since I bailed out of the cruiser I had been trying to repossess. Three days since the *owner* shot it out of orbit.

The light moved down the length of the cocoon leaving a trail of molten metal-plastic ooze behind it. I had no idea what the cocoons were made of, but it had done its job. A fall from orbit without a parachute, and I was still alive.

:: 3 ::

As the seam of light grew longer and longer, the pressure on me began to ease, and I felt more and more of my injuries. I'm amazed, honestly, that I even stayed awake that long.

The saw stopped.

The cocoon cracked open.

I looked into Alice's bright gold eyes.

"Welcome home," she said.

The pain throughout my broken body erupted and overwhelmed me.

I don't remember any part of the next three weeks.

··2··

The first breath I took when I woke was free and easy. The second, even easier. But with the third, a globule of phlegm dislodged and I broke into a hacking cough.

"Whoa, whoa, he's awake," said Alice. "Help me sit him up."

It felt good to hear her voice.

It didn't feel quite as good to have two pairs of hands reach behind my shoulders and push me to sitting. It hurt like hell.

It did help the cough, though.

"That hurt," I growled. More growl than normal. They must have only recently pulled the breathing tube.

"Sorry, Grimm," said Alice.

I liked hearing her apologize. It didn't happen very often.

"How long?" I asked.

"Three weeks."

Damn. The bastard was probably three systems away by now.

"Why aren't you after him?" I asked.

"Who says we aren't?"

I opened my eyes, slowly. I had been putting that off, knowing that the bright lights of the hospital would hurt, and I wasn't ready to deal with that, too.

We weren't in a hospital, and someone had done me a favor and kept the lights low. Probably Alice.

It took me a moment, but when my eyes adjusted, I recognized the medic bay of the Grim Repo.

"Thanks for getting me out of the cocoon. I don't know how much longer I would have lasted in there."

"By the amount of air left in the tanks, I think you had about thirteen minutes, give or take," she said.

I didn't bother to say thanks again. It wouldn't matter to her.

I looked behind me. Mickey and his over-muscled physique stood, bulging arms crossed, almost.

"You cut me out?" I asked.

"No, Renaldo did. Alice had me searching for that asshole."

"You find him?"

"Yeah. We're about a day behind."

"Where are we going?"

"Stantion."

Holy shit. We'd been through eight systems already.

"He's really running, isn't he?"

"He's not even stopping to refuel. He's got to be running out soon."

"Good," I said, turning to look at her. Very good. I don't know why he shot me out of the sky, but I don't like it when people do that. "We get a kill order?"

"First thing."

She'd probably applied for it before coming to look for me. Synths were always 'job first'.

I made a note to ask her about it later.

"Can we get me out of here, then? I'd like to see what's up."

"Tests first," Alice said.

Right.

▪ ▪ 3 ▪ ▪

About three hours later, Alice declared me fit enough. Fit for duty really doesn't count much on this ship. All I had to be able to do was sit in my chair, lift my arm high enough to tap screens if I wanted, and survive moderate g.

It hurt like hell to walk up there, though.

"I thought you said I was fit," I said to Alice as we walked the one corridor that ran nearly the length of the ship.

"You are. The only fractures you have left are hairline and should be sealed in the next eight hours. I had to rebuild some of your musculature, which could lead to some tenderness. A few days, and you'll be working like normal."

A few days would probably keep me out of any of the fun stuff when we found this guy.

As I entered the bridge, Renaldo and Eddy turned to see who was entering. When they saw it was me, I got a short round of applause. I couldn't tell if it was sarcastic or not.

Renaldo grinned, his lips exposing his teeth. His black hair barely escaped the gravity of his scalp, he kept it so short. Green eyes blazed like fire emeralds.

"Good to see you, Captain," he said. "Next time, you oughta take a course before you pilot one of those things."

"There wasn't time," I said as I settled into my chair. My muscles ached from just the small exertion of walking to the bridge. I secretly wondered if they'd had to reconstruct them all. "What I should have done was have *you* pick up that ship."

"You'd never let me."

He marked me with that one. I enjoy the pickup. I won't let anyone else do it.

"That was one pretty explosion, though," said Eddy.

Eddy was smiling, too. Unlike Renaldo, her smile wasn't full of mirth. She had a thing for me. I knew it. I didn't exactly know how to handle it.

She was pretty enough. Straight brown hair framing a delicate face with huge, dark eyes that saw everything around her. Smart as hell, too, and the best marksman on the crew.

But for some reason, I couldn't return her interest, and trust me, it wasn't because I held to some sort of professional code when it came to relationships. I didn't.

GRIM REPO

Alice has never been shy in suggesting that I might have lower turnover on this boat if I refrained from fraternization, but I live on the Grim Repo. I don't trust most women on station, and I don't trust any woman planet-side. I tell potential crew members about my policy and suggest that if they don't like it, they probably shouldn't fly with me.

And I had told Eddy.

I had thought that there might be a possibility, which is one of the reasons I hired her, but when the opportunity came, I didn't take it. In two years, I haven't taken it.

"What do you think was on board that made it so pretty?" I asked her.

Some disgruntled former owners try to take out their ships through sabotage or other means, but they usually fail. They're not terribly insistent once they get return fire from the Grim.

But this guy had wanted that ship gone.

"I don't know. I've got an analysis running on it, have had it running since we got you back aboard, but I haven't been able to identify it, yet. It wasn't any of the more common explosives."

I tapped my desk, and it blinked on. The Grim Repo logo came up while it prepped my screen. I guess no one had taken my chair while I'd been out.

"How far, now, Renaldo?"

"We're five hours to the Stantion portal."

"He go through already?"

"About sixteen hours ago."

"Does that mean we're catching up to him?"

"Slowly," said Alice.

I looked up, and she was standing next to me.

"We're gaining about an hour every twenty-four."

And we'd lose a couple hours on the other side of the portal while we worked to pick up his trace. The worst kind of chase.

But it would be worth it.

"What's the bonus on the kill order?" I asked.

"Ten mil."

"The bank doesn't like Mister Ehfrain, do they."

"I wouldn't want to speculate," said Alice. She never wanted to speculate. I assumed it was her nature as a Synth.

"You don't have to. I can speculate just fine. The bastard didn't break that part of me."

Ten mil was more than the normal kill order bonus. Significantly more. Enough to make me suspect Mister Ehfrain owed them for more than just the ship we'd been hired to repo.

They'd want him back alive, of course, if it was possible, but since he had proven unreliable at making his payments already, the bank would take it out of his hide, and probably safeguard any other assets he might have that the bank could obtain from his estate.

I decided to do a quick check into Mister Ehfrain's background, see if there was anything we had missed, if he had any other publicly acknowledged assets, or even assets that weren't so publicly acknowledged.

I entered a dozen queries asking for every public record about the delinquent, batched them up, and sent them off. Then I started another batch of queries, which I sent off to some friendly resources that could help find less than public information, along with enough untraceable credit vouchers to pay for their help.

"You're using Elliot again?" Alice asked.

"He helped us last time," I said.

"He almost got you killed, last time."

"His information was accurate. We wouldn't have found the guy without it."

"His information was incomplete and put you in the precarious position of trying to repo the ship in the middle of a local turf war that involved the delinquent."

My stomach rumbled.

"How was he to know? Those things flare up all the time." Of course, Elliot should have known. It was his job.

I pushed myself up out of my seat.

"Where are you going?" Alice asked.

"To feed my empty stomach, and then to take a nap. Wake me after we're through the portal."

I shambled past her and off the bridge.

She really had done a number on me.

No.

That wasn't right.

 It was Ehfrain that did the number.

And I was going to make sure that next time, I'd have a number for him.

But first, I needed to eat.

··4··

I felt the transition to Stantion in my sleep. I always do. And it always wakes me up. This time, the slight wrenching feeling felt a lot stronger and made my bones ache. I put it down to my recent exploits with free-fall.

I waited to see if Renaldo or Eddy would call down to wake me up. That's what I told myself. In truth, I had no desire to get out of bed until I was needed. Working my reconstructed muscles would probably help them heal, but lying in bed was much easier.

"Captain," the call came through from Mickey, not Renaldo. "You're needed on the bridge."

Dammit. They called, and it wasn't a wake-up call. What the hell had gone wrong, now?

I limped to the bridge as quick as I could. Three minutes wasn't bad, considering the complete lack of exercise I'd had with my new muscles. I was out of energy by the time the hatch opened.

"Why the call?" I asked as I made my way to my chair.

In answer, several screens popped up on my desk. Two, at first glance, looked like empty space, but a closer look showed a debris field. Each screen had a different view. The remaining screens showed trace analysis, particle analysis, and whatever else Mickey thought I should see.

"What am I looking at, other than a debris field?"

"We think it's Ehfrain's ship. There are ID markers throughout. It's still hot."

Damn.

"Authorities?"

"No contact yet."

"Where's Alice?" She would know what to make of this disaster.

"She's running a drone through the field."

I looked away from the debris filled screens and tried making sense of the other data Mickey had sent to my screen.

The particle analysis didn't show any sort of explosive residue or weapons fire, but there were some strange readings I hadn't seen before.

"Eddy, I'm looking at the particle trace. What am I looking at?"

"I don't know, Captain." Everywhere else on my ship, I insisted on Grimm. But on the bridge, I insisted on Captain. "It looks very similar to the pretty explosion you survived."

"And you don't know what that is, yet?"

"It's not in any of our databases, and the computer hasn't come up with a composite match, either."

I went back to studying the screens, and checked out the ship trace. There were several ship traces, which wasn't surprising this close to a gate. But Mickey had highlighted two in particular.

One he'd marked as Ehfrain's ship. It showed the path out of the gate, and the trace led straight into the debris field.

The second, he'd marked with a big question mark.

The trace originated near the debris field, and then led away. The origin had a time marker that coincided within twenty minutes of the arrival of Ehfrain.

But it didn't have an entry trace, not from the gate, not from in-system. It just seemed to have appeared. Traces are visible for days.

"You're quiet, Captain," Mickey said. "You lookin' at the ship trace?"

"Yeah." I explained what I saw. "Did I miss anything?"

"Nope. What do you think, Captain?"

I think I wanted Alice up here with me, because what I thought scared me a lot more than I wanted to admit. I wanted her to tell me I was full of shit, but I didn't think she would.

Still, I banged on the com. "Alice, to the bridge."

"You can't figure it out, Captain?"

MARK FASSETT

I looked up from my desk, out across the bridge. Mickey had spun in his chair and was looking at me.

"No. I think I've got it figured out. I want her to tell me I'm wrong."

·· 5 ··

Alice bent over my desk and looked at the trace.
"I've already seen this," she said. "That's why I had Mickey send for you."

"Your conclusion?"

She looked from the screen to me with her golden eyes. "That you should see it."

"Why can't you, for once, just tell me what I'm looking at?"

"It's not as much fun as shooting you down when you're wrong."

Great.

"Okay, here's what I think," I said. "Ehfrain bugged it here because he has a partner. The partner waited for him, picked him up just as he was about out of fuel, and then they blew the ship, hoping we would think he was dead."

"You think he's still alive, Captain?" Mickey asked.

"We can't discount the possibility. That other ship waited here for days. It knew Ehfrain was coming."

"Maybe it was someone else wanted in on the bounty."

I sighed. "I don't think so. You said Ehfrain was skipping refueling stations. I think he knew someone was waiting for him. It makes me think..."

I didn't want to believe it.

"What does it make you think?" Alice asked.

"It makes me think Ehfrain knew we were coming."

"Of course he knew we were coming," Eddy said. "He was behind on his payments."

"No. I think he knew exactly when we would make the repo attempt. Otherwise, how would he be in such a perfect position to shoot me down?"

And from there, the implications really took on all sorts of sinister colors. A mole in the bank? On my ship? Who would stand to benefit?

"You're not saying anything, Alice."

"I have nothing to say. Your analysis is sound."

Fucking great.

I looked up at my crew, my employees, and wondered if any of them had tipped Ehfrain off. I hadn't hired anyone new in twenty months. I felt pretty certain they were all tight and the leak didn't come from within my ship.

But why would someone at the bank leak my timetable?

The answer was easy.

Money.

But if Ehfrain didn't have the money to pay for the ship, where did he get enough cash to bribe a bank employee? Hell, where did he get the money to run additional ships, to self-destruct them and have someone wait for days in the dark to pick him up?

Those questions would have to wait.

"Find anything with the drone?" I asked.

"Bits and pieces," said Alice. "The ship ident tag, some samples of various unknown materials."

"Let me know when you figure out what they are," I said. "Mickey, follow the trace."

"It's heading to Stantion Prime."

"Planet-bound?"

"Yes, without any deviation so far."

"Time frame?"

"Two days."

"Follow it."

The engines pumped to life and the slight g shift as we accelerated pushed me back in my chair. The grav unit on board could only compensate for so much.

"And Eddy, get us in contact with Stantion authorities. We need to let them know we're here."

"On it."

I felt a presence at my shoulder, and I looked up. Alice was still there.

"Something to say, Alice?"

"Shouldn't we report this to the bank?"

"Not yet, Alice. There's something going on here, and I don't want to get edged out of our kill bonus."

I also didn't want to let the bank know I suspected they had a mole. If they didn't know, they couldn't tell Ehfrain, and I thought I'd need every advantage I could find to bring him in.

··6··

There's something about exercising on a treadmill that bores the crap out of me. Oh, yeah, walking in one place.

Unfortunately, it's about the only exercise you can get on the ship that isn't strength training, and Alice's prescribed therapy precluded anything that might stress the bones in my arms and legs. No curls, bench presses, nothing. Except walking.

It did let me think without too much interruption, but that wasn't always good for my state of mind.

It was fortunate, then, that Elliot's data had come in just before my scheduled therapy session. I had something to review while I walked.

Before the data, there was a message from Elliot.

"Grimm, glad to hear from you. I heard you had a serious case of the explodes. I'd hate to see you splattered across the universe.

"Here's all the data I could find on your man. His

record is cleaner than Alice's language, but we both know that a man with that kind of money made mistakes somewhere, especially if his boats are getting repoed. The only thing I can figure is he's got connections.

"Say 'hi' to Alice for me, Grimm, and watch yourself. A man with connections like this guy won't like to be cornered."

I grunted. No shit. I knew that first hand.

I wiped some sweat from my forehead then decrypted the data. After a few moments, the file spread open on the screen, and I discovered what Elliot said was true. There wasn't anything in it that looked out of place. No arrest records, warrants, not even a mention of his debts. It was hardly any different than his public file.

It made me wonder. Did Ehfrain have connections with Elliot, too? Was it a warning?

Footsteps approached from behind me. I turned my head a bit to see who would interrupt my therapy.

Eddy, clad in a gray tank-top and black, hip-tight shorts, waved at me and smiled.

"Hi Grimm, I didn't think the treadmill was your thing," she said as she climbed onto the other tread-mill and started walking with me.

"It's not. If I'm going to walk, I want to go somewhere."

"You can always turn on the sim," she said.

I smiled. "Hardly the same thing."

"What's on the screen?"

"Ehfrain's profile, courtesy of Elliot." I tried to look at her face, but the walking made her chest heave just a little under the tank-top and I couldn't help but look. I wondered, not for the first time, why I hadn't made a move on her. She seemed willing, my eyes were willing, but the rest of me—I couldn't figure out the rest of me.

"Anything useful?"

"Only one thing. The debt is not listed. It's off the books. It looks like it's been scrubbed."

Eddy frowned. It drew her forehead down when she did it.

"That shouldn't be possible. Didn't you once tell me debt records are supposed to be tamper-proof?"

That made me forget I was on the treadmill, momentarily, and it nearly pulled me over when my feet stopped walking.

"They are tamper-proof," I said, once I regained my balance.

"Then the other conclusion is that the debt was never listed in the first place, right?"

This time, I stopped the treadmill before I stopped walking.

"If it wasn't listed in the first place, then..."

I didn't like what I was thinking.

I commed the bridge.

"Renaldo."

"Yes, Captain?"

"What's our time to target?"

"Fourteen hours, now. They land in thirty-four hours at their current velocity."

Fourteen hours behind them right this minute. If we boosted, seriously boosted, we could cut that in half, but they might rabbit.

"Are they at their maximum thrust?"

"I don't think so, sir."

And any data on that would be several minutes old, anyway.

"Do you think we could catch them if we boosted?"

"Maybe, but I doubt it. You wouldn't want..."

"No, we wouldn't want to go hot into Stantion Prime. I'm just thinking."

And I wasn't thinking anything good.

"What's the trouble, Grimm?" Eddy asked. She had stopped walking, too.

I punched the comm again, only this time ship wide. "I want everyone in the mess in five. Not you, Renaldo. I'll comm you in."

I picked up a towel and dried off before I replied to Eddy.

"I think we're being conned."

··7··

Eddy followed me to the mess, still in her exercise outfit. Alice showed up just after we did, and Mickey trailed in last.

I sat down at the table and hit the comm so that Renaldo could listen in. Everyone else took seats, too.

"Here's our status. We're chasing Ehfrain down to Stantion Prime. He's boarded another ship we haven't identified, yet. I got the data back on Ehfrain, and it looks like he had it wiped. There's nothing to use against him anywhere in it. The interesting thing is that there's no record of his debt, either.

"When we came through the portal and found his ship in pieces, I started to think we had a mole, that someone had told him we were coming."

"A mole?" Eddy asked. "No one here would..."

"No, at the bank. But with the debt missing from the records Elliot gave us, I suspect it isn't just a mole at the bank. I think someone gave him that loan off the books."

Even Alice blinked at that.

"You think our contact at the bank set us up?" she asked.

"Maybe. Who is our contact?"

"Russel Agners. I think he's a Senior VP."

I nodded. That sounded right.

"So how often does a Senior VP get involved in a repo?"

"They don't," said Eddy.

"Right. They don't, unless the debt is significant..."

"Or they made the loan off the books," said Alice.

"Who gave us the kill order?"

"Russel," said Alice

Her face went slack. She was thinking through everything, like I had at the treadmill.

"The kill order isn't valid," she said, when she came back to herself.

"And if we kill him?" Mickey said.

"We go to prison, or worse, for murder."

The table went silent for long moments while everyone thought it over.

"Captain," Renaldo said over the comm, "I've got an ident on the ship that picked up Ehfrain."

From the sound of his voice, I could tell I would not like the answer to my next question, but I had to ask.

"What is it?"

"Black Dog."

Black Dog. I knew the ship. I knew the captain. And I knew she had been sent to clean up our mess.

"How can this get any worse?" I asked, and then wished I hadn't.

"I've got a message coming in from the Black Dog," Renaldo said.

"That's how," said Alice.

If she wasn't a girl, I would have hit her.

8

I took the transmission in my cabin. I wanted to negotiate with the captain of the Black Dog in private. I never knew what she might say, and I sure didn't want some of the things she knew about circulating among the crew. As soon as I had the transmission routed, I encrypted it. One of the privileges of being the captain and the owner of this tub. It would all get stored to the data core, anyway.

Mira's face still had that spark that attracted me to her. Curls framed her face, though she had cut the back shorter than I preferred it. Her thick lips and high cheekbones gave her a look that advertising types would love to capture.

I smiled, thinking about what might happen if someone proposed that she become a model. The person that suggested it might be lucky if they only ended up in the hospital.

"Grimm," she said by way of a greeting. "I'm hoping that it's you I'm talking to. I can't imagine that ship running around the universe without you."

This conversation looked like it would be fun.

"Mira. Glad to see you're still alive. What's on your mind?"

There was about a thirty second delay before I received her reply. In the meantime, I watched her face, trying hard not to stare into her eyes. She'd see that. She'd probably think I wished we were still together.

"I saw you pop through the gate and stop to examine your surroundings. It's a shame you had to find out that way that I popped your man."

Dammit. She *was* waiting for him. Russel had somehow put her on this, too. I tried not to look upset. I didn't want her thinking the wrong thing.

"I hope he's still alive," I said.

Thirty seconds later, she said, "He's still alive, but I don't imagine he'll live long. You better take care, too. The bank seems a bit put out that you didn't nab him back on Akers, and still haven't tracked him down."

I felt like strangling something. The ache in my muscles, especially in my back, was returning.

"You've gotta keep him alive, Mira. Your contact at the bank wouldn't happen to be Russel Agners, would it?"

I tried to massage my back unobtrusively. I didn't want her to know how badly I had been hurt. If there was one thing I didn't want her to see again, it was me being vulnerable.

"That's exactly who it is. Why do you care if we keep him alive? You're out of it, now."

When Mira went out on her own, this was exactly the sort of thing I feared would happen to her. She always liked to take contracts at face value.

"I did some poking around after Ehfrain bugged out. The loan from the bank was never recorded. It's an off the books loan, and if Ehfrain turns up dead, whoever had him last could end up wanted for murder. If you give him to Russel and Ehfrain ends up dead, you are an accessory."

That was long enough. I waited, impatiently tapping my fingers on the desk.

"What are you talking about, Grimm? Russel's a Senior Vice President."

"Check yourself. The loan is not on the books. Did you do a particle scan of the debris? Did you see the explosion?"

"No. The explosion was something else, though."

"Ehfrain was transporting something with his ships. A new weapon system, some other sort of explosive, I don't know. I had Elliot check Ehfrain out for me. He came up clean. *No one* comes up clean."

She wasn't smiling anymore, at least.

"Are you sure you're not trying to fly yourself back in to this claim?"

"No. I think something stinks. Russel gave us a ten mil kill order. I want you to be careful Mira. I think anyone who turns Ehfrain in could end up just as dead as Ehfrain." And I thought anyone that even knew of Ehfrain and his connection to the bank might end up that way as well.

There were far more than thirty seconds of transfer time before I got a reply. She seemed to be thinking, her eyes staring into the screen. Maybe she was trying to decide if I was telling the truth.

I was about to say something else when she said, "All right. I'll be careful. Tell me why I should trust you."

I tried not to let my outrage show. She was the one that had lied throughout our relationship. I didn't mind, honestly. It made it exciting.

"Before your call, I was trying to figure out how to get Ehfrain back so I could put the Feds onto Mr. Agners. I'd already given up hope of getting paid for the job."

"Fine. I'll slow our approach some so that you can catch us. If he's as hot as you say, I don't want to be on Stantion on my own. Tell Alice I said hello."

"I will," I said. "It's good to see you."

It wasn't. But I had to make sure we maintained some civility. My life and my freedom were more important than screwing Mira. Not that I'd mind taking her to bed one more time, just for old time's sake, but I'd have to check for knives, first.

I shut off the transmission, and slammed my fist against the desk.

"She's still got you on her mind," Alice said, making me jump. She'd snuck in during the conversation. That was what Mira meant by her Alice comment.

"She does."

"She doesn't really want our help," said Alice.

"No, she doesn't. She wants us close enough that we can't make a move without her knowing what it is."

A smile grew on Alice's face, her golden eyes giving her a cat-like look. One of the few times I'd ever seen her smile. Of course she would think this was funny.

"She learned from the best," Alice said.

Of course she did. She learned from me. Right at that moment, I regretted teaching her.

∎∎9∎∎

We caught up to the Black Dog about twenty-three hours later, still a day out of Stantion Prime dock control. Mira's ship was about two thirds the displacement of the Grim Repo, but what it lacked in size, it made up for in sleekness with its thin profile and recessed weapons bays. That it wore black didn't hurt its looks at all.

I suspected that it might be capable of a ground landing, which the Grim Repo couldn't even think of doing. Its profile would also make it tougher to shoot at, though it couldn't pack nearly as many armaments as I could.

In short, it was an extension of Mira, just like the Grim Repo was an extension of me.

And when I said we caught up, what I mean is that we got within a few thousand kilometers. There was no reason to get closer, even if she would have let us. Too close, and there was little chance of retaliation or avoidance, not that I thought we would start shooting at each other, but it wasn't out of the realm of possibility, especially if she somehow concluded I was trying to sneak Ehfrain off her ship to collect the fee for myself.

I settled into my chair on the bridge, tapped my desk and waited the few seconds for it to come back to life. My bones felt better. They didn't ache anymore, but my muscles still hurt, and sitting in one place too long made them start to cramp.

"Have we heard from Stantion Prime, yet?" I asked.

"The usual," Eddy said.

The usual, which meant an inquiry as to our intention to dock.

"You answered in the affirmative?"

"I did."

Well, that was out of the way. It wouldn't look too good if we had to change our plans, but the dock needed enough warning. They didn't like undeclared visitors.

"What's the Black Dog been up to?"

"They've matched our velocity and are running a parallel course."

"You've got weapons trained on them?"

"Trained, but not locked, like you ordered."

"Good."

Now, it was up to me.

I set up a secure communication link to the Black Dog and waited for Mira's response.

She came on almost immediately.

"I've been waiting for you to call," she said.

She had her hair pulled back this time, so that you could almost not see her curls, but for the few that had escaped their binding.

"Did you have a chat with Ehfrain?"

"He's not very talkative."

"You didn't get anything?"

She shook her head. "Not anything useful. As soon as I told him we suspected the loan was off the books, he clammed up."

"That's unusual."

Mira started saying something else, but my mind drifted down channels, wondering why he would clam up. And then I had it.

"He thinks we're Feds, or at least, that you're a Fed."

"What?" She looked surprised.

"It's the only explanation for him clamming up. He thinks you're a Fed and that you're playing him for whatever it was that he was smuggling in his ships. I want to come talk to him."

The tip of Mira's tongue slipped out between her lips, which always happened when she was deep in thought.

"Fine, but only you."

"Alice, too."

"As long as it's not Mickey. I don't want that brute on my ship."

"Done. See you in an hour."

"It will be good, Grimm. I've missed you."

I laughed. "No you haven't."

She smiled, and then the connection dropped.

"Alice," I sent through the comm. "Meet me at the shuttle."

"You really think this is a good idea, Captain?" Eddy asked.

I pushed myself up out of my chair, every muscle groaning, before I answered.

"No, I don't think it's a good idea, but I need to talk to Ehfrain before we dock. I want to see that asshole face to face."

An hour and a half later, I docked our shuttle to the Black Dog, and Alice and I floated through the short docking tube that Mira had extended for us.

I never liked going through those things. They always felt fragile, but the Black Dog was too small to take the shuttle on board, so I had little choice.

Handholds extended into the passageway about where the Black Dog's internal gravity field kicked in. They allowed you to keep your head up and let your feet sink to the ground as you crossed the grav threshold—kept a person from looking like a fool.

By the time we reached the hatch, our feet had settled to the floor, and we had weight again. It was heavier than I was used to. I had forgotten that Mira was from New Terra, and preferred a stronger gravity field. I guess she had energy to burn. I preferred to run lighter and save money.

"Tell me why I am here with you," Alice said as we waited for the hatch on the Black Dog to open.

"I want you to keep an eye on Mira for me. I want you to make sure she's not pulling some scam on us that I can't see."

"You never could see the truth about her."

The hatch on the Black Dog slid open at that moment, and I had to hold back my response. I didn't want Mira to know we were talking about her, though she probably had bugged the tube. I should have kept my mouth shut. Alice would have paid attention to Mira, whatever I wanted.

The opening hatch revealed Mira in her black ship-suit. The top of her head came up to my nose. I guess she decided she didn't need to wear heels as the Captain. She had a pistol in a holster on her thigh. She didn't trust me. She had two of her crew behind her, both a head taller than her, and neither looked terribly friendly.

I ignored them.

"Mira," I said.

"Grimm," she said. "It's been a long time since we were face to face."

"It has."

"You said some unkind things the last time."

"I wasn't the only one," I said, hoping she wouldn't take offense, hoping she'd grown out of her anger some, or at least grown up.

"No," she said. "You weren't."

So she had learned how to put her anger aside. I wondered how long she could keep it there.

"How are you, Alice?" Mira asked.

When Alice didn't answer, Mira said, "Still angry at me, I see."

"I don't get angry," Alice said.

"No, I guess not. You should try it some time. You might learn something."

Mira turned back to me.

"So you want to see our guest. Come on," she said and then turned around, motioning her muscle out of the way.

I followed her through a half dozen cramped passages, the price she paid for having the smaller ship, until she led me to a cabin. The door was locked.

"Is he free to move about in there?" I asked.

"He has a tether. He can do what he needs to, but he can't get near the door."

She punched the lock on the door, and the door slid open.

I looked inside.

The cabin was small, like the rest of the ship. A bunk was built into the far wall, facilities to the left. One end of a tether was attached to a clip that had been welded to the wall between the bunk and the facilities. The other end was attached to a man that appeared to have been asleep on the bunk until we opened the door.

Ehfrain sat up. His hair was quite a bit greasier than when I'd seen him last. He hadn't bothered to take a shower in a while. His ship-suit was torn. He'd struggled, it seemed.

But the fake smile that he always seemed to wear made an appearance almost as soon as he realized it was me in the doorway and not one of his captors.

"I'm amazed you're alive," he said.

"Why so amazed?" I asked.

"I didn't think you had time to get out."

So he had missed the cocoon ejecting.

"Why did you try to kill me?"

There was a chair at a built-in desk near the door. I wanted to sit down, take the strain off my muscles. I should have thought about what the extra gravity would do to me.

But I didn't dare. I wasn't ready to make friends with Ehfrain, yet.

Ehfrain shook his head from side to side in answer to my question.

"What do you mean?"

"Not with them here," he said.

I looked behind me. Alice, Mira, and Mira's two goons stood just outside the door.

"Mira," I said.

"I get the hint. One hour."

Mira signaled to her two goons, and the three of them left.

"Her too," Ehfrain said.

"She's with me."

"I'm not talking with a Synth around." I wondered how he knew she was a Synth—you can't tell by looking at them. I could only guess someone had told him.

I examined the tether. It looked strong enough. I doubt Mira left him with anything dangerous. I would have checked more thoroughly, but I wanted him to trust me.

"Alice..."

She stepped out and closed the door without saying anything.

For good measure, I reached in my pocket, pulled out a jammer, flicked it on, and set it upright on the floor. It would nullify the obvious bugs. The more sophisticated ones would still leak our conversation. Unfortunately for Ehfrain, the jammer was also a recorder.

But Ehfrain seemed satisfied. He sat a little more upright.

"So, why try to kill me?" I asked again.

"I wasn't trying to kill you. I just couldn't let that ship leave."

"Why?"

His eyes shifted between me and the jammer. He was trying to decide how far he could trust me.

"Look, you're not with the Feds, right?"

"Right. I'm purely a businessman. I take contracts

to repossess items when the debt on those items hasn't been paid."

He reached up and wiped at his nose.

"Okay. That ship was carrying some cargo that I couldn't let fall into the wrong hands."

"Mister Agners' hands?"

"Among others."

"What was the cargo?"

He squinted. "Why are you asking all these questions?" he asked.

"All right, let's forget that one for the moment. It doesn't really matter. Did you know that your loan from Harper Galactic Bank was not on the books?"

"What do you mean?"

I finally gave up. My muscles were killing me. I grabbed the chair and sat down, still out of reach of Ehfrain. I didn't think he could hurt me, normally, but the way my muscles were aching, he might have had a chance.

"I mean, Ehfrain, that after you tried to kill me, I did a little deeper research into your background. I discovered that the person who approved your loan at the bank never recorded it."

"Shit."

"Yeah, shit. That man wouldn't have been Russel Agners, would it?"

He nodded. I think he could see where I was going.

"Well, you blew up his ship. The ship he would

have sold to cover his ass at the bank. He gave us a shoot-to-kill order, Ehfrain."

"But I had the goods, I just needed to offload them, and I would have paid him."

"It was too late for that, Ehfrain. Why didn't you just unload the goods from the ship? You knew we were coming."

"It was part of the deal. I needed that ship, that particular ship. I'd made some modifications." He rubbed the back of his thumbs, like they'd recently been hurt. Probably during his escape, or extraction, from the wreckage of his ship.

"You had your other ship." I really could have used a drink and some pain killers. The ache was starting to reach the back of my head.

"My other ship didn't have the modifications yet. I didn't have time. That one was the demonstration. Look, just let me go, and I'll get him the money."

He'd slipped, and almost confirmed my suspicion.

"You don't think I can just let you go, do you? Russel's going to pay me ten mil to kill you."

"What about the Feds?" he asked. "You're on their ship."

I laughed. It was so funny, it almost hurt. He really did believe they were Feds.

"What's so funny?"

"They're not Feds, Ehfrain. They work for me."

Ehfrain shook his head. "No, man. I know they're Feds."

"Look around. They've got you locked in a cabin. If they were Feds, they'd have you locked in a cell, and they'd all be wearing Federation uniforms. Mira? I taught her all she knows." I couldn't imagine Mira as a Fed.

"They're under cover," he said, but his hand started to tremble.

I leaned in close to him, closer than advisable, Alice would say. "Ehfraim, if they were Feds, do you think they'd let me in here alone to talk with you?"

Apparently, I'd convinced him. His eyes grew wide with fear. He was looking past me, trying to decide if he could get out, probably forgetting about the tether.

"Don't...don't kill me. I...I can get you the money, more than that!"

"How? Your ships are blown, your cargo's gone. What can you do for me?"

"Please..." He sounded like he was going to cry.

I couldn't allow that. Not at all.

"Grow a spine, Ehfrain. Tell me what the cargo was, who you were selling it to, how much. Give me all the details, and maybe we can work out a deal."

"A deal. You won't kill me?"

"That's up to you."

He was beginning to piss me off. How had a guy

like him become wealthy enough to command a two-hundred mil loan? Really? How did he survive long enough without getting caught?

"All right. The cargo was a new weapons system. I needed the ship as a test platform. I had it outfitted with these special cannons that could deliver this tiny little package ten million clicks. I don't know how it worked, exactly, but this package could not be detected by any current anti-weapon systems, and it delivers an explosive that penetrates shield systems like they aren't even there."

"Like a nuclear weapon?"

"No. Nukes can be tracked, destroyed at range. This stuff will burn through shields and hulls in microseconds."

And that's why Eddy couldn't identify it.

"Where'd you get it?"

"The Fringe."

Fucking great.

"Don't bullshit me, Ehfrain."

"I'm not. There's a whole bunch of rogue weapon-designers out there. The Arcers support 'em."

"They can't do anything this sophisticated out there," I said.

Fuck. I needed out of this shit, out of the room. I reached down, picked up the jammer, then stood up while trying not to let my aches show.

"I've got ten mil coming my way that says you're a

dead man, Ehfrain. Tell me why I should believe you. Tell me how you're going to get me enough cash to leave you alive."

Ehfrain's eyes flitted back and forth, looking for an escape that didn't exist. If he wrung his hands together any harder, I expected I'd hear the popping of bones.

"I've got another ship. One more load of the goods. If I can get it to my buyer, it's worth a hundred fifty mil."

"Where?"

"I tell you, you'll go take it for yourself. No way."

He was right about that, but not for the reasons he thought.

I flipped off the jammer and tapped on the door to let Alice know I wanted out, assuming the internal controls were disabled.

The door opened.

"Please!" Ehfrain said.

"I'll think about it."

··11··

"So," Mira said as she sat across the tiny mess table in her galley, "what do we do?"

"I don't think it's a good idea to dock with him on board, but it's not safe to float around out here, either," I said. "I think Agners knew what was on board that ship when he ordered the repo."

"You think he wants it?"

"I do."

Next to me, Alice sat silent, observing. Mira's goons left when Mira shooed them away.

"So, what do we do? I didn't take this job to waste my fuel."

"I'm open to ideas. We can't turn Ehfrain over to Agners because Agners will just kill him, and likely us. He might have a hit out on both of us right now."

"I would," Alice said.

"So we can't sit here. Did you message Agners that you picked Ehfrain up?"

Mira nodded, her curls flipping over her eyes.

"The pickup point is on Stantion?"

She nodded again. I hated her when she got like this. When she parceled out bits of information like they were her last credits.

"And you were going to tell me when?"

"If it ever became necessary."

This was precisely the type of thing that resulted in her either quitting or being fired from my ship, depending on whose story you believed.

"Dammit, Mira, this stuff is necessary to know!"

"That's why I answered you."

"Were you meeting Agners?"

"He said he would send someone."

"You're supposed to die there, you know."

She brought her eyes up to look into mine. It was always hard to look away when she did that.

"So you say. I'd rather believe that he's a man of business, and that he would honor his contracts."

Contracts. Dammit. Were our contracts recorded with the bank?

I stood up. I had a burning need to message Elliot again. And I needed to talk to someone else at the bank besides Mr. Agners. If our contracts weren't on file with the bank, then our own part in this could be brought into question were the Feds ever to get wind of it. It wouldn't surprise me if they had never been filed.

Mira stood up when I did.

"Where are you going?" she asked.

"Back to my ship. It seems you're intent on taking your chances with Agners. I'm not."

She stepped around the table, put her hand on my chest. "What will you do, Grimm?"

"I'm going to figure out a way to keep me and my ship out of the fallout when you drop your package off."

"You're not interested in the weapon?"

"Why would I be? I'm not an arms dealer."

"He offered you a lot of cash."

I reached up, grabbed her arm, pulled it away from my chest. She was after something, and I wasn't going to let her have it, whatever it was.

"What I do is legal, Mira. Always has been, always will be. I don't want the Feds pinching me for arms dealing. I don't want the Feds pinching me at all. You be careful. If Agners doesn't kill you, and the shit falls on him, don't be standing too close."

She wrested her arm out of my hand.

"Take my advice, Mira. Dump the man some-where. You can't kill him without a valid contract. That would be murder. But you can dump him wher-ever you want. Don't take him to Agners."

"It was good seeing you, Grimm. I'll consider your advice."

I knew what that meant. She'd toss it and do whatever she wanted.

Fine. She wasn't under my command anymore.

I made my way out of the galley, back through the tube and into the shuttle. Alice never left my side, and she never said a word. Not until the door closed and we were disconnected.

"Something's wrong with her," she said. "It didn't feel right."

"I know."

She was too nice, too accommodating, even if she wouldn't take my advice. For the first time, despite the fights, the bad blood between us, I feared Mira Solano.

··12··

I needed a plan. My first thought when I returned to my ship was to message the CEO of Harper Galactic. Explain everything to him. But I couldn't know whether or not he was in on the scam, too.

My second thought involved telling the Feds everything and letting them sort it out. But I quickly decided that wouldn't work out the way I wanted, either. They would seize the Grim Repo until they could decide whether I should be charged as an accessory. That would mean my employees could be out of work for months, if not years.

I needed something better.

I needed a plan that would erase me from the entire mess like I wasn't even there.

Better, one that saw I got paid.

I couldn't see my way around it, and now, with us only being eighteen hours out of dock with Stantion Prime, we had to dock.

I decided a shower and a nap would help, and left Alice to service the shuttle.

Back in my cabin, I took my shirt off and sniffed it. Shower first. As a bonus, it would soothe my aching muscles.

Fifteen minutes later, I lay down in my bunk, my hair damp, and relaxed into the receptive gel mattress.

After a moment, I got up, pulled the jammer / recorder from my discarded shirt, and plugged it into my desk. I set it to play on repeat and went back to my bed.

And I listened.

I thought I would fall asleep.

But listening to the interview had the opposite effect—it kept me thinking about what I'd heard.

And one line from Ehfrain kept jumping out at me.

"What about the Feds? You're on their ship."

Over and over.

It made me think back to the conversation with Mira, where we had been talking about how Ehfrain had clammed up when they tried to talk to him. Mira had been so surprised when I suggested Ehfrain thought she was a Fed.

Surprised that I figured out what Ehfrain thought?

Or was it something else?

Holy shit.

I jumped out of my bed and punched the comm in my desk for Alice.

"I thought you were sleeping."

"I've got it," I said, standing there naked despite being aware she could see me—at least, some of me.

"Got what?"

"Mira's a Fed."

And I had to wonder how long she had been a Fed. Had she been one while she was aboard the Grim Repo? Had she been one while she was in my bed?

The spot in the back of my head that had given me pain since I can remember, that no doctor had ever been able to fix, started to ache like it always did when I couldn't put the puzzle pieces together.

"It makes sense."

"What?"

"She provoked you. She wanted you to fire her. She needed off your boat, and if she quit, she might have to answer questions."

"What does that have to do with now?"

"She seemed rather nice to you today, don't you think?"

I nodded. Too nice, business-like, but not angry about the past. Even at the end, where she all but refused to listen to my advice, she was still far more pleasant to me than I would have expected.

It made me wonder if there still might be something there.

The back of my head ached, I needed sleep, and I was thinking about Mira Solano.

"You're too quiet," Alice said.

"Sorry, thinking."

"She's a Fed, Grimm. We ought to turn and run. Nothing good will come of following her down to Stantion Prime."

"We don't have a choice," I said, back to thinking about our problem. "We've been assigned a dock. If we run, it'll look like we're trying to hide something."

"Aren't we?"

"No. We're trying to keep Agners from putting a hit on us, and he will, once he gets his hands on Ehfrain. When he gets the weapons, he'll want to ice anyone who knows about them. He's got to figure we know by now."

"So how do we do that?"

"I thought you might have an idea."

She frowned. Almost an actual emotion from her.

"Fine. We've got some time. Let me sleep on it."

"That's what you were supposed to be doing when you called me."

"Wake me in six," I said.

I flicked the comm off and climbed back in my bunk without turning the interview back on. This time, I'd try the relative silence of a ship decelerating as it nears dock.

··13··

A buzz from my desk brought me awake, but none too fast, and it seemed, far too soon. The ache in the back of my head still throbbed. I checked the clock. Only three hours had passed.

I crawled out of my bunk and went to the desk.

"Why am I awake?" I asked.

"Incoming message from Russel Agners," Renaldo said through the comm.

Great. I probably looked like hell.

"Did you tell him I was asleep?"

"I did. He asked me to wake you."

I scrounged up a shirt and dragged it over my head before I sat down. I didn't want him to see the lower half of me, though I thought it amusing that he would be talking to me while I was half dressed. It seemed appropriate, since he had caught me with my pants down on this whole fiasco.

When Russel's image popped up on the screen, I said, "Hello, Mr. Agners."

The man was dressed in a dark suit with a thin collar. The same suit I'd seen him wear every time we met. I was pretty sure the thin gray tie was the same, too. His hair was as gray as his tie. He looked every bit the buttoned up straight arrow he had looked the first time we talked about this contract. I should have been suspicious, then, but his dress and demeanor put me off. He was looking off to the side at something, probably another screen, while he waited.

About thirty seconds later, his eyes came back to look at me, though he was looking at the me of fifteen seconds earlier. "Mr. Grimm. Glad to see you're in good health after the mishap."

Thirty seconds. I checked the clock. We were about fourteen hours from docking at Stantion Prime. This wasn't any call routed through a gate. The man was on Stantion Prime.

"Thank you," I said. "Sorry I couldn't keep the delinquent from destroying the property."

I had to give Mr. Agners credit. He knew how to look interested, even though he would be waiting for thirty seconds for a reply. I don't have that skill.

"It was unforeseen," he said, "but I reviewed the documentation your people sent me, and it didn't look like there was much you could do about it. Now, the purpose of my communication with you is to inform you that we will still honor the expenses portion of your contract, but, of course, cannot pay the completion portion. The kill order has also been rescinded as I've been informed that another party has apprehended the delinquent.

"As it happens, I am on Stantion Prime for a meeting, and if you would like to pick up your payment, I'd be happy to meet with you in person. I'll even buy your crew a round for their efforts in tracking him down after the mishap."

I tried to keep my face from changing expressions as I listened. I didn't want him to suspect that I already knew about his scheme.

And his claim to bring the payment personally—a load of shit. All he had to do was drop it in our account.

"They'll be excited to hear that," I said. "We dock in about sixteen hours. I'll message you when we're down."

He probably already knew when we were scheduled to dock. My lie to him, I hoped, would either be taken as truth, or would mask what I really intended to have Renaldo do.

"That'll be fine. I'm looking forward to it. Now, I have another call. I must go."

The screen winked out.

Rude. But not uncommon when dealing with a thirty second lag. I could have sent one last message, which would have been forwarded to him, but I didn't care to do that.

I commed Renaldo.

"What's up, Boss?"

"Push our pace, Renaldo. Get us into dock as quick as you can. I don't want that asshole waiting for us."

I wavered in my chair a bit as additional thrust kicked in.

"One other thing. Wake me when we're three hours out."

I really needed to sleep.

··14··

The space station that served as the primary dock for Stantion Prime was not the largest station I had ever seen. In fact, it was among the smallest. Stantion Prime was a backwater system, but a limited amount of traffic still found its way there. The planet had a large population and did brisk trade with other systems, but it was off the major trade routes. It didn't have to support much pass-through traffic.

If I didn't know Russel Agners was trying to clean up his mess, I would have wondered why he was there. I wasn't even sure if Harper Galactic had a branch on Stantion.

The dock operation went as well as could be expected, three hours ahead of schedule. The Ops Manager of the station messaged us and asked us why we had to hurry. I fed him a lie that our contact on planet needed to move our meeting up.

They got it done, though they charged us a

surcharge, but I didn't care. I just hoped Russel Agners hadn't paid any dock workers to inform him of our early arrival.

I had fully expected Mira to accelerate to match us, or at least message me and ask what the hell I was doing, but she did neither. I didn't know what to make of it. Either she was waiting to see what would happen to me, or she was waiting to see what move I made, or she didn't give a shit about me at all.

When the engines were shut down, the ship buttoned up, I had everybody gather on the bridge.

Mickey and Eddy sat in their chairs. Alice stood next to me, and Renaldo leaned against the bulkhead.

"I know most of you know something about what's going on, but I want to make sure you all have the details.

"The ship we were supposed to repo..."

"The one you blew up," Mickey said and laughed.

"Yes, that one. It was carrying a stolen, experimental weapon system that can shoot through shields at ten million kilometers. Currently, there exists no defense against it, if I'm understanding correctly."

Renaldo let out a low whistle.

"Yes. Some bad shit. Now, Russel Agners, our contact at the bank, loaned the money to our delinquent off the books. I suspect Russel and our delinquent were in business together, and that they had some sort of falling out, because Russel is here on

Stantion Prime. I don't think our contract to bring in our delinquent was ever valid."

"If it wasn't valid, then..." Eddy started.

"If it wasn't valid, we are technically guilty of attempted robbery on a capital scale. That we were subsequently given a ten mil kill order is just a bonus ass fucking."

"Glad we didn't get him," Mickey said.

"Yes, we're fortunate that didn't happen. Unfortunately, Mira picked him up, and I have reason to believe she's a Fed."

Both Mickey and Renaldo looked surprised by this. Eddy hadn't known Mira, but those two had both worked side by side with her.

"Did she become a Fed after she left us?" Mickey asked.

I shook my head. "I don't think so."

"Let me see if I've got this straight," said Renaldo. "We've got a renegade banker using us to pop one of his guys that's running arms for him, a Fed that has the guy that was running arms, and we're all here, or going to be here, on Stantion Prime."

I nodded. "It gets better. Mister Agners invited us out for drinks so that he can pay us for our expenses."

"Shit." More than one of my crew uttered that expletive.

"I'm betting he has plans to kill Mira, too. The

delinquent claims to have another cache of weapons worth upwards of a hundred-fifty mil," I said.

"What are we going to do?" asked Eddy. She started chewing on her lower lip after she asked the question.

"I'm open to ideas. We have to somehow avoid getting killed while keeping our asses out of prison. If we can, I'd also like to keep the Feds from getting those weapons. I have little hope of that, however, unless they're in-system."

"Well," said Mickey, "that's not much to ask."

We sat there, quiet for a time, each in our own thoughts.

"I've got an idea," said Renaldo. "Why don't we meet Mister Agners, kill him, then get off station before anyone is the wiser?"

In my gut, I liked the plan. It was simple.

"The are only a couple minor problems with that plan, Renaldo. First, he's already planning to kill the lot of us, so I'm guessing we'd be far outnumbered in any meeting we set up with him, if he even decided to show his face. Second, getting off the station before anyone knows he's dead is likely to be difficult. He's a Senior Vice President of Harper Galactic. Men like that have protection and alarms. In the time we have, we aren't likely to sever all of those links. I do like the idea, though. I've wanted to put a bullet in his brain since I discovered we were being played."

It's always good to tell your employees you like their ideas, even if you don't. It makes them think you're listening and keeps them working to come up with ideas. Sometimes, you don't even have to lie.

"Why don't we just wait for the Fed to come and pick him up?" asked Eddy.

"I don't think he knows she's a Fed, and I'm sure he's planning to kill her as soon as he gets his hands on Ehfrain."

"But won't she be planning for that?"

"I'd like to think so, but it still leaves us with the issue of what happens if she fails to detain him. He'll still put out a hit on us."

"Why don't we help her?" Alice asked.

Help Mira. Help the Fed.

"It would leave the Feds with access to those weapons."

I didn't want to help her. After she forced me to fire her, to find out she was lying to me all along, lying to me even now, to find out she was a Fed. I didn't trust her. I didn't want anything to do with her.

Except for one thing.

I wanted to know why she was crewing on my ship. Who was she after?

"Are you going to believe a man that would do anything to escape the Feds or the death he has to know is awaiting him for destroying that arms shipment? He wanted off that ship, Grimm. Don't let your feelings about Mira or the Feds get in the way of using your brain."

I looked up at Alice. Her golden eyes were looking down at me, waiting for an answer.

And she was right. What were the chances that there was a third shipment of those weapons hidden somewhere?

I tapped my desk, brought up the report on Ehfrain that we'd received from Elliot.

I scanned through it, looking for the number of ships he purportedly owned. When I found the section, it listed only the two ships—the one he had destroyed with me in it, and the one Mira had destroyed with him in it. There weren't any other ships registered to him.

He could have had ships registered under another name, but he had come up clean. Elliot didn't miss aliases.

"You're right Alice," I said. "The chances he was bluffing are greater than the chances he knows of another shipment. And it won't matter if the Feds get this shipment or not, assuming it exists. If they don't, they'll get another. Those weapons came from somewhere. They're out there. What matters is digging us out of this mess."

Alice actually smiled.

"So what are we going to do?" asked Mickey.

All that wasted fuel to get here early, just so we could wait around.

"Mickey, I want you to tap into the station camera feeds. I want an idea of who is watching us. I want the rest of you to prep the ship for departure while we wait for Mira to arrive."

"What then?" asked Eddy.

"Then," I said, "we're going to give her some help."

··15··

Docking with a station brings a few benefits, one of which is that access to remote data stores is much quicker. I don't have to rely on people like Elliot to do my data mining for me. Elliot was good, but I didn't want to put him on to Russel Agners. Elliot sometimes sold information he found to others. Usually that didn't bother me, but I didn't feel like letting Elliot in on this cargo.

I retired to my cabin, brought up my desk, and hooked into the local feed.

The first thing I wanted to find out was how Russel had come to be on Stantion Prime. He couldn't have followed us. He couldn't have slipped past us. We would have discovered his trace. He couldn't have followed Ehfrain, either. He'd been here ahead of the two of us. And he'd known where to send Mira.

So my first query was for docking records, passenger manifests, anything with the name of Russel

Agners or Harper Galactic attached to it. Some of the data would be public record—ship transit records, for instance. But passenger lists and the like were held in encrypted databases behind firewalls and layers of security. They were normally hard to get at, if not impossible.

Unless, of course, you had Federation codes. The Feds required access to those databases at all times. If you had codes, or could impersonate an agent to get the codes, you could get access to those databases.

One of the benefits of being the captain of my ship was that I had access to data about my employees, including those long terminated.

Like Mira.

In the past, Elliot had given me codes. This time, I thought I would try to impersonate Mira. She was in-system, and I knew she was a Fed. Knowing what she was working on, more or less, there wouldn't be too many flags if she looked up information on Russel Agners.

I found Mira's old biometric data, eye scans, fingerprints, and fed them through my desk to the blind relay Elliot used when impersonating a Fed. Elliot had told me once that it looked like a Fed computer, and pretended that all requests originated from it. He'd cautioned me that it would eventually get discovered if used too much, but that didn't bother me. It wasn't my computer, and I knew Elliot had to have backups.

GRIM REPO

After about twenty minutes, the codes that I needed came back. I have no idea how transmissions go that fast when passing through multiple gates and across who knows how much space. I've heard it said that the gates can transmit data instantly between gates in the same solar system, which would mean that you're only waiting for the time between the gates and the terminals, but I've never heard it confirmed. The Gate Corporation kept that information secret.

I plugged in the codes and found myself logged in to the transit records on Stantion Prime.

I limited the search to within four gates of Stantion and to the last ten weeks. Only people on the run pushed their fuel limits like Ehfrain did.

The data-sets started coming in almost immediately. The first sets contained the local information. I combed through the data as it came in.

Ten minutes later, I found the first piece of information I needed. Russel Agners arrived on Stantion Prime two weeks earlier, just a week after Ehfrain destroyed our target. It surprised me. I had thought Russel would hide his identity, but perhaps a man in his position didn't think he had to hide where he was going.

But, I had my first supposition confirmed.

Russel Agners knew where Ehfrain was going.

The question was, how did he know?

I let the query continue to run. It might be able to tell me where he came from, and I felt that might matter.

I started a new query that was a bit more targeted. I found my records on our original target ship. I also found the records that Elliot had sent me about the other ship Ehfrain had owned.

I ran them through and queried for previous owners, repair records, impounds—anything that might help. This one would take awhile. It didn't require any special codes. It was all public information, and it was a query I ran often when searching for a ship that had disappeared. I didn't have to run it on Ehfrain's ship before because it had been right where Russel had said it would be.

I should have wondered how he knew where it was.

I ran to the galley to get a turkey sandwich, then came back and ate at my desk while I looked through the results of the first query.

The sandwich was tasteless and bland. I made a note to talk to Renaldo about our food sources.

For the most part, the data contained little of interest. It seemed there was a branch of Harper Galactic on Stantion Prime. There was quite a bit of Harper Galactic traffic through all the systems in the query. What I had hoped to gain with that hadn't panned out. Instead, I was buried in a mountain of useless information.

GRIM REPO

I looked at the clock and saw that I didn't have enough time to resubmit the query. I'd just have to hope I'd find the pebble I needed in that mountain.

My comm buzzed.

"What is it?"

"Russel Agners," said Mickey.

"Put him through," I said, regretting that I had to do it. He must have learned we'd landed early.

"Grimm, you landed and I didn't hear from you."

The man was smiling—the smile of a predator.

"We've been busy," I said. "Had some things to clean up. We'll be done in a couple hours."

"Ah, I see. Nothing I like to see more than a captain who runs a tight ship."

I had to work extra hard to keep from scowling. I didn't imagine the man had ever spent time working on a ship.

"I'll tell you what," he said. "Meet me in two and a half at the Aten Club. Bring all your crew. Like I said, I'll buy a round."

"Looking forward to it," I said and forced a smile.

I hoped he thought it was genuine.

My second query finished, and the desk spit out a bunch of information. I couldn't stop myself from reading.

The first screen of data contained the ownership history of both ships. Scanning through, I saw that both ships had changed hands several times very recently. But the original owner of each ship was Russel Agners.

"Is something wrong, Grimm?"

"What?" I looked back to the screen and tried to remove the scowl that I knew my face had fallen into.

"Is something wrong? You look like you saw something you didn't like."

"Oh," I said. "Someone just sent me some maintenance records and it seems there's a problem that needs to be addressed."

"Ah."

"I'm sorry I couldn't keep myself from looking at them until we had parted."

"Quite all right. We'll see you at the Aten."

"Good bye, Mister Agners."

The transmission ended, and I exhaled.

Russel Agners hadn't loaned Ehfrain the money for the ships. He'd loaned the money for the weapons.

But if he'd loaned Ehfrain the money for the weapons, then why had he sent me to repo the ship?

Unless Ehfrain had planned to sell the weapons himself, or Russel had.

I punched the comm.

"Mickey. Get me connected with Mira. I need to talk to her."

"On it."

Maybe Mira knew this information, but maybe she didn't. I thought she might be walking into a trap if she was still thinking of Russel as just the financier, and I had to warn her.

··16··

I watched the Black Dog dock from the bridge. The ship was sleek, I had to give Mira credit for that. It slid in without even an adjustment. The grapples reached out and connected, pulled the ship tight to the station.

She was here.

And she hadn't responded to my transmission.

Alice, for once, was sitting at her station instead of hovering over my shoulder. "Alice, can you get us a feed of the communications coming from Black Dog?"

"I can try," she said, "but if Mira really is a Fed, it won't be easy."

"Just try."

I had to hear what she said to Agners.

"Uh, Boss, they're leaving the ship," said Mickey. "Looks like they've got the delinquent with them."

Shit. It was already too late. Having Mickey tap into the station camera feeds when we docked was paying off. It wasn't technically legal since we didn't have a valid contract. Hell, it wasn't technically legal even with a valid contract, but it was a lot more defensible in court, and it might just save our asses.

"Give it up, Alice. I need to know where they're going. Mickey, Renaldo, time to weapon up."

"Ahh, yeah," said Mickey.

"I knew this was coming," said Renaldo.

I shut off my desk and stood. "Don't sound so excited."

"What about me?" Eddy asked.

It would be nice to have her with us. An extra gun to even the odds, but the ship needed two people to fly it, and I had a bad feeling we might be leaving in a hurry. Agners, presumably, had enough men to take care of all five of us.

"I want you on the ship, ready to boost us out of here if we come running back with heat on our asses."

She looked disappointed. "I can shoot better than Mickey."

"Not this time. I'm hoping to get away with just breaking heads."

Mickey and Renaldo left the bridge to hit the weapons locker.

"Take care of the ship, Alice."

"Don't get *your* head broken."

"Lock the door when we leave. Don't open it for anyone."

Then I ran off the bridge and caught up with Mickey and Renaldo. They were already raiding the weapons locker.

I dug in after them and pulled out my weapons belt, which was preloaded with a pair of Geary pistols and a dozen magazines. I grabbed the comm earpiece and jammed it in my ear, then pulled on a carbon-titanium mesh jacket that would keep most shipboard rounds from entering my chest. It wouldn't keep them out of my head, but I was counting on Agners' goons to try for the sure hit.

"Where are we going, Alice?"

I led my goon squad off the ship, and then shut the hatch tight.

"Looks like they're headed to the core of the station. It's a bit strange, though. The hallways look deserted."

"Come on," I said to Mickey and Renaldo, and led them out of the docking bay and into the outer ring.

The station did look deserted. We'd already dealt with the customs officer, but there still should have been some operations personnel wandering around.

I ran for the closest corridor that would take us to the core.

Usually, station designers put operations at the core, kept them safe from docking mishaps. But Stantion Prime's dock housed the premium entertainment venues there. I've never figured out why.

"Looks like she's got six armed men with her," Alice said.

"I wish I could ask her what she's doing. Why the hell is she bringing Ehfrain with her? If she's a Fed, and if she's after Agners, why risk her only possible informant?"

The running was taking its toll on my newly reconstructed muscles. I had to slow down, or I knew I would be worthless when we got to wherever we were going. I just hoped we wouldn't be too late.

"You gettin' old, Boss?" Mickey asked.

"No, it's that bangup job you guys did reconstructing me. I think you put the pieces in backward."

The two of them laughed.

"I just received a message from Mira," Alice said.

"What'd she say?"

"I'll forward it to you."

Moments later, I got a beep on the mini-desk built into the sleeve of the jacket, and tapped it. The audio was routed to my earpiece.

Mira's face appeared on the screen.

"Don't follow me, Grimm. I'm trying to save your ass."

Then it blinked off.

"Fuck. Why won't she let me have a conversation with her?"

"Because she knows you don't take 'no' for an answer," Alice said.

"That's not fair, Alice."

We stepped on a moving walkway. There still wasn't anyone around. I wonder who had set that up—Mira or Agners. If Agners had done it, we were in deep.

"They've stopped moving," Alice said.

"Where are they?"

"Just outside the entertainment area. Looks like she's directing her men to spread out. She's keeping Ehfrain and a pair of her gunmen with her."

"How far are we behind them?"

"Three minutes," Alice said. "If she doesn't move in two, you're going to want to get off the walkway or you'll run right into her."

"Like hell I'll get off. I want to talk to her."

I took a deep breath, then eased into a jog on the walkway. The muscles in my legs and in my back yelled at me to stop, threatened to cramp up, but if I wanted to stop her from going in, I didn't have a choice.

Of course, I'd probably arrive late, anyway.

"She's moving, Grimm," said Alice.

Dammit.

"Where?"

"She's entering the club Agners mentioned to you, the Aten."

So Agners had planned to take care of business with Mira before finishing off my crew. I pushed the pace, but I knew I would be too late.

"Hold up, Grimm," Alice said. "She's inside with Ehfrain. The four men she left outside might see you."

"And mistake me for Agners' men. Got it. But I need to know what's going on in there." I slowed up, though, and stepped off the walkway to the side. I was thankful she made me stop. My muscles didn't want to work any more.

"Wait a minute. I'll see if I can get a feed."

I could see the end of the corridor from where I was, but I couldn't see the Aten, and I couldn't see any of Mira's men.

I crept forward. Mickey mirrored my position on the other side of the walkway. Renaldo stayed behind me.

"Let me know when I'm in danger of being seen," I whispered.

"I think I've got a feed. It's from a camera across the corridor. There aren't any in the club that are accessible."

Not surprising. Clubs didn't want the Feds, or anyone, peeking in on their customers. I'd have to get us in there before things went to shit.

"One of Mira's men is walking your way," Alice said.

A quick search of the corridor revealed no place to hide. He was going to find us and either arrest us, or start shooting. I didn't want to shoot back. As much as I dislike them, killing Feds isn't exactly the best way to stay alive.

"Be ready to lay the guns down," I said into the comm.

"Wait," Alice said. "There are several men slipping out of a storeroom. They're armed."

Not Mira's. "Feds? Station security?"

"I don't think so."

Agners' men. I hadn't heard any shooting yet.

"What are they doing?"

"They're coming up on one of Mira's Feds now."

I heard the first shot. The bark of a pistol rang through the corridor.

"Your man is running to help his partner," Alice said.

More shots.

I peeked around the corner. They were on the other side of the Aten. The Feds had taken up positions along the walls, behind vending machines and a couple portions of the wall that jutted out into the corridor. I couldn't see their attackers.

"How many?" I asked.

"Eight."

I saw a clear path to the Aten. I had no idea how many were inside, but with Mira's men outnumbered, if I dashed in to save her, I might not get back out.

I had to tell myself that I wasn't trying to save her. I was trying to make sure that Agners ended up in prison or dead.

Which meant that I had to make sure Mira's Feds lived.

"Does this corridor lead us around the bend, Alice?"

"It does," she said.

Time to run again.

I slipped out of the corridor and sprinted across to the far wall. I motioned for Renaldo and Mickey to follow.

Then we sprinted, as fast as we were able, through the corridor.

"Let me know when to pull up," I said to Alice between puffing breaths.

We passed several shops as we ran through the corridor that circled the core. All of them were closed. Agners had a lot of pull here. What else had I missed?

It didn't matter now.

My back started to ache, and I had to slow a little.

Gunshots still rang through the corridor. They weren't all dead yet.

"Alice?"

"Just a little further."

"I can't go any further," I said.

I pushed myself, though. I couldn't let the Feds lose, or I'd lose.

"Pull up," she said.

It was almost too late.

A bullet ricocheted off the far wall and zinged past my ear.

"What's the status on the Feds?" I asked as I knelt down against the wall.

"One is hit, but he's still shooting. The others still seem to be okay. One of Agners' men is down, too. He's not shooting."

I started creeping around the wall. Mickey and Renaldo followed.

I pulled out a pistol, held it in front of me. I carry the second in case something goes wrong with the first. I'm not one of those vid guys that can run around shooting with a gun in each hand.

As soon as I saw the first of Agners' men, I pulled the trigger, putting a round in the man's back.

He fell to the deck. I didn't think he'd get back up.

One of his friends leaned over to check him.

I put a bullet through his ear.

Mickey jumped out from behind me and started shooting.

They hadn't prepared for an attack from the rear.

He put two more down, and then ducked behind a trash receptacle.

By my count, that left them with three. A fair fight.

Renaldo slid out from behind me, shot over the top of Mickey, and put down another of Agners' men.

Two still standing.

They threw down their weapons.

"Weapons down, hands up." I heard the shouts.

"Don't shoot, don't shoot!"

Their hands went up.

"You too, Captain Grimm."

Fuck. They knew we were here, and they knew who we were. That wasn't good.

We didn't have much choice, though.

"Drop 'em," I said while I let my gun belt slide too the ground. I placed my pistol next to it.

Renaldo and Mickey were still laying weapons on the ground when I stood up and placed my hands in the air.

"Step out where we can see you." It was hard to hear over the ringing in my ears.

I moved out from the wall as unthreateningly as possible. Mickey and Renaldo followed my lead.

One of Mira's men had already stepped over the makeshift barricade of knocked over vending machines and was cuffing the two of Agners' men that were still standing. Of the five men we had put on the floor, only two appeared to be alive. The sixth man down, the one the Feds had shot, had fallen over on his side and blood had pooled under his head.

Another of Mira's men stepped past him and came toward me.

"Captain Grimm," he said.

I had seen him before. He was one of the goons that had escorted me aboard Mira's ship.

I nodded. I couldn't remember his name. I wasn't sure I had been told what it was.

"I'm supposed to cuff you and sit you down out here until this is all over," he said.

"Did Mira tell you to do that?"

The Fed nodded. "But I've got a man down, and these two here, and the two on the ground. I can't keep an eye on all of you and keep her safe, too. And I should thank you for helping us out."

"That part was my pleasure," I said. It was. I don't like people who try to screw me out of my ship and my money.

"What do you want?" I asked.

"Can you sit out here, watch these four, call for a medic? We're going to..."

The sound of gunfire escaped through the cracks in the door to the Aten Club.

The Fed said, "Stay here," then spun around and ran for the Aten with his two uninjured cohorts on his heals.

"Like hell I will," I said, and went back for my weapons.

My ship and my crew were at stake, and I wasn't going to let the Feds lose either of them for me.

··17··

The Fed and his pals went through the door of the
Aten without looking back.

The injured one had managed to sit himself up. He
had his weapon trained on the two of Agners' men
that had been detained.

"Go, help them," said the Fed. "I've got these."

He deserved a medal. As I passed, I saw his leg had
a field wrap on it. He'd be all right.

I jammed a new magazine in my pistol as we ran
for the door.

Shots from inside the club still rang out regularly.
No one was talking in there, I suspected. That part
was over. I did wonder who still lived. The only one I
cared about was Mira. If Ehfrain died, if Agners died, I
was all right with that.

Mira needed to live to prove I'd been duped.

We held up right outside of the doors. There were
bullet impacts in the safety glass. Even inside the

station, most of the glass would hold pressure and stop anti-personnel rounds. But the glass wasn't designed to take round after round. Eventually it would give out.

Which was why I didn't just stand there. Instead, I poked my head up so I could see through the glass, then ducked back down again.

"See anything?" Renaldo asked.

"Nope. A whole mess of smoke in there," I said. "I think most of the lights are out, too."

Not an ideal situation.

Another round hit the window and it shattered, raining glass down on me.

I pushed the door open slowly, sliding it in its track. Either the motor was out, or it was one of those retro do-it-yourself type of establishments.

Bullets came our way. Someone didn't want us inside. I didn't think the Feds would shoot before knowing their target, so my bet was on Agners and his men.

"Mickey, can you snake a camera through there?" I asked.

"Sure thing."

Mickey scooted around me, then pulled a remote camera from his jacket pocket, slipped his hand through the opening we had made, and stuck the back of the camera to the door. The cameras were small, no larger than a button, but they had a remote feed back to the ship, and they adjusted to light levels automatically. They were great for spying on a delinquent, figuring out his patterns. They were also good for getting a better visual in a gunfight.

I typed a code into the screen on my arm, and the video from the camera showed up. I couldn't see anything right away, it was too dark, but after a moment, the camera adjusted to the light level and gave me a good view of the room just inside the door.

Tables had been turned over, used as shields. There were several men on the floor, all either dead or incapacitated. One was right inside the door, probably one of the three Feds we had just saved. I could just make out Mira behind a table about a third of the way across the room from us. She had two men with her. One looked like it might be Ehfrain, the other was probably a Fed. I couldn't see Agners, but that didn't mean anything. Much of the room was out of the current viewing angle.

"Alice," I said.

"You all right? I haven't heard from you in a while."

"Fine. I need a direct link to Mira," I said.

"I'll do what I can."

I wouldn't be able to get a link if she wasn't wearing a comm, but I can't imagine she'd go in to something like this without one. Besides, she'd sent me a message already, and it didn't sound like she'd prepared it ahead of time.

"What do you want, Grimm. I'm busy."

"We're right behind you, at the door."

On the screen, I watched her poke her head up, fire off a couple rounds at someone at the far end of the room, then duck down again.

"Is it only you, Ehfrain, and one of yours?" I asked.

"Yeah, the others are down."

"How many hostiles?"

"Four, I think."

Mira's Fed peeked around the edge of the table and fired several shots before ducking behind it again.

"Including Agners?"

"I assume so. Are you coming to help, Grimm? I don't have time to chat."

"Where do you want us?"

"There's another table along the wall to your right. Can you see it?"

"Hold on."

I tapped on my screen, adjusted the camera to the right until I saw the table she was talking about. It was on its side like hers, only the men who had been behind it were out of commission.

"I see it."

"On my mark, get yourselves to that table. We'll cover," she said.

Bullets flew our way again.

I motioned to Renaldo and Mickey that we were moving to the right, and showed them the table on my screen, then waited.

"Go," Mira shouted.

At that moment, she and the other Fed played several rounds across the far end of the room.

I shoved the door open and ducked inside, running as quickly as I could while my overworked muscles shrieked at me.

I rolled over behind the table, on top of a pair of Fed bodies, making room for Renaldo and Mickey behind me.

Gunfire came our way, but it missed its mark.

We were safe for the moment.

I looked down at my screen and saw it had gone blank. I'd crushed the camera when the door opened.

"Another camera Mickey, on the other side of this table."

He got it out, readied it.

I waited for a lull in the gunfire, then put my hands over the top of the table and started firing. "Now!"

Mickey snuck his hand around and attached the camera to the table.

Then we both ducked back down.

With luck, Angers wouldn't spot the camera and we'd get a good look at his layout.

After a moment, I had an image on my screen.

Agners and his men had taken refuge behind the bar. The ceiling appeared mirrored, but the screen was too small to get a good idea of what was going on behind the bar in that mirror. We'd have to get closer.

"They're behind the bar," I said into my comm.

"Yes," said Mira.

"Is that you, Grimm?" Agners shouted through a momentary break in the firefight.

"I thought you were buying us drinks," I shouted back. "I just came to get my money and be merry."

"Sorry about that," he said. "This little lady here turned out to be a Fed, and she's trying to arrest me."

"For what?" I asked.

"Corporate fraud, of all things. I'm the Senior Vice President at Harper Galactic. Why would I defraud my company?"

"Why, indeed," I said in a whisper not meant for his ears.

"Don't listen to him, Grimm," Mira said into my ear.

"Are you really after him for corporate fraud?" I asked her.

And then I shouted, "I haven't a clue. All I want is my expense money, since she took my delinquent."

"Yes," Mira said. "He's defrauded Harper Galactic of billions."

That was Mira. Always seeing the planets, but not the system.

"If you help me out, Grimm, I'll pay you for the entire contract," Agners said.

I didn't believe that at all.

"Mira, he's after Ehfrain because they were in business together running those weapons. As far as I can guess, Ehfrain tried to sell the guns on his own. That's why Agners went after him. Both of those ships were sold to Ehfrain by Agners."

"What do you say, Grimm?" Agners asked.

"I don't know. Killing a Fed is dangerous," I said.

"Only if they live to talk about it."

Renaldo tapped me on the shoulder, then pulled out a foam grenade from inside his coat. We use them for rapidly sealing off areas of a ship. They explode this sticky mess that hardens into solid, fire resistant foam in seconds.

I muted my comm. "You brought those?" I asked in a whisper. I wish I'd thought of it, but then, preparedness was one of the reasons I kept Renaldo around.

He nodded.

"How many?"

"Three."

"Hand them out," I said.

Renaldo handed me the one he was holding

I released the mute on my comm.

"Mira," I said.

"What happened. Why are you negotiating with this guy, Grimm?"

"Go with me on this, Mira."

Mickey and Renaldo each had their grenades ready.

"Did you try to bribe her, Agners? I know she's crooked as all hell," I said.

I heard Mira gasp in my comm.

"She wouldn't take," Agners said.

"You probably didn't offer her enough. Did you tell her about the weapons?"

"What weapons?" I heard a hint of surprise in his voice.

"You know, the ones Ehfrain was selling for you, or would have if he hadn't tried to sell them on his own."

I readied my grenade.

"What are you? You're not a Fed. I checked you out."

"Ehfrain said there's another cache of those weapons somewhere. He messaged you while he was on the run, told you there was another cache. That's why you hired the Fed here to steal Ehfrain from me."

"Did he tell you about them? Wait. You're with her?"

"Now," I said.

I pulled the pin on my grenade and threw it towards the bar. I tried to get it over, but my reconstructed muscles betrayed me. It landed just in front.

Renaldo's and Mickey's, however, were perfect throws. Their grenades landed on the other side of the bar.

"Grenade!" I heard someone shout.

"What the hell, Grimm?" I heard in my comm from Mira.

Then they exploded one after another just as Agners and his men tried to escape.

They didn't get far.

··18··

Two days later, and after what seemed like ten thousand interviews by the Feds and the security branch of Harper Galactic, I finally got to sit down in my chair on the bridge and order us to undock.

I couldn't say I'd miss Stantion, and Harper Galactic gave us a small reward for helping bring Agners to justice. It wouldn't cover our expenses, but it was better than nothing, and they gave us another contract, this one guaranteed legal. I did my homework this time.

"Transmission from Mira," Alice said.

She was the one Fed I hadn't talked to in the last two days. The other Feds wouldn't let me near her, which was probably for the best. She hadn't been too happy at having to cut herself free of the foam after my grenade went off and foamed everything in front of the bar, including her hair, which had apparently been sticking up above the edge of her table at the time. She really should have been wearing a hat to protect her hair, or ducked a bit lower behind the table.

I took the transmission there on the bridge.

"Mira," I said.

She didn't look half bad with a buzz cut.

"They're finally letting you out of here, I see."

"I've got another contract," I said. "What about you?"

"I don't know. I think they're contemplating putting me on a Federation cruiser for a while. My cover's blown."

"But you got your man," I said.

She smiled. "I did, and I got more than I expected. We had no idea he was the one actually running the weapons. We thought he was just providing loans."

"Well, I'm glad I could help. I do have one question, though," I said.

"What is it?"

"Why did you spend time aboard the Grim?"

"I had to establish my cover," she said.

"So all business."

She laughed. "Not all business. You weren't the worst employer I ever had."

"Thanks," I said. "If you ever need a spot..."

I couldn't believe I had just said it, but I had. I was willing to give it another chance, now that I knew she had forced me to fire her on purpose.

"That's nice of you," Mira said, "but I don't think Alice would let me put one foot on the Grim."

I laughed. "Probably not. Careful out there."

"You, too," she said.

She reached below the screen and the transmission ended.

"Take us out, Renaldo," I said.

"Yes, Captain."

The docking clamps disengaged with a thunk that sounded throughout the ship. A bit of thrust, and we were drifting free of the dock.

"You would let her back aboard this ship?" Alice asked.

"Why not?"

Alice gave me a stern look, then turned back to her desk without answering.

Maybe she was right. Maybe it would be a bad idea.

But then again, maybe it would turn out different.

After all, she'd only tried to steal the Grim Repo out from under me in order to solidify her cover.

"Take us to the gate, Mickey," I said. "We've got a starship to repo."

ABOUT THE AUTHOR

Mark Fassett lives in western Washington with his wife, children, and cats. He's had extensive experience in the mobile game business and was involved with some of the top selling titles at the time of their release, including multiple Duke Nukem Mobile games and Guitar Hero World Tour Mobile. He's also played and written music most of his life, and was "this close" to actually making money at it.

FIND ME ONLINE

Blog
http://www.markfassett.com

Twitter
http://twitter.com/mark_fassett

Facebook
http://www.facebook.com/markfassett.writer